Heidt

DICKENS LIBRARY

David Copperfield

by Charles Dickens

abridged edition

Published in Great Britain by World International Publishing Limited.
P.O. Box 111, Great Ducie Street, Manchester M60 3BL.
Printed in The G.D.R. SBN 7235 7659 9.

My Early Life

Whether I shall turn out to be the hero of my own life, or whether that station will be held by anyone else, these pages must show. To begin, I record that I was born on a Friday, at twelve o'clock at night.

I was born in Blunderstone, Suffolk, a posthumous child. My father's eyes had closed upon this world six months before mine opened on it.

The first objects that assume a distinct presence before me, as I look back into my infancy, are my mother with her pretty hair and youthful shape, and Peggotty, our servant, with no shape at all, and eyes so dark that they seemed to darken their whole neighbourhood in her face.

What else do I remember? Let me see.

There comes our house. On the ground floor is Peggotty's kitchen, opening into a back-yard; a pigeon-house without any pigeons in it; a great dog-kennel in a corner, without any dog; and a quantity of fowls that look terribly tall to me.

I remember the parlour, where Peggotty and I were sitting one night by the fire, alone. I had been reading to Peggotty about crocodiles. I was tired and sleepy; but having leave, as a treat, to sit up until my mother came home from a neighbour's, I would rather have died than have gone to bed.

At last the garden bell rang, and we went to the door; and there was my mother, looking unusually pretty, I thought, and with her a gentleman with beautiful black hair and whiskers, who had walked home with us from church last Sunday.

He patted me on the head; but somehow, I didn't like him or his deep voice, and I was jealous his hand should touch my mother's in touching me—which it did.

"Let us say 'goodnight', my fine boy," he said.

"Goodnight!" said I, and he shook my hand heartily, and went away. I saw him turn round in the garden, and give us a last look with his ill-omened black eyes, before the door was shut.

We spent many happy days in our home, the three of us, walking in the garden and sitting in front of the cosy fire by night. Then gradually, I became used to seeing more of the gentleman with black whiskers, Mr Murdstone, who often came to call upon my mother.

Shortly after he started calling, Peggotty said to me, "Master Davy, how should you like to spend a fortnight at my brother's in Yarmouth? Wouldn't *that* be a treat?"

The day soon came for our going, and we set off, Peggotty and I, in a carrier's cart, which after many hours finally reached Yarmouth, which looked rather spongy and soppy, I thought.

We were escorted by Ham, a relation of Peggotty's, towards the seashore, until we came out upon the dull waste, when Ham said: "Yon's our house, Mas'r Davy!"

I looked in all directions, but no house could *I* make out. There was a black barge, high and dry on the ground, with an iron funnel sticking out of it for a chimney; but nothing else in the way of a habitation that was visible to *me*.

"That's not it?" said I. "That ship-looking thing?"

"That's it, Mas'r Davy," returned Ham.

I was charmed by it. There was a door cut in the side, and it was roofed in, and there were little windows in it; but the charm of it was that it was a real boat which had been upon the water hundreds of times.

We were welcomed by Peggotty's brother, a hairy man with a very good-natured face. "Glad to see you, sir," said Mr Peggotty. "You'll find us rough, but you'll find us ready."

I thanked him, and replied that I was sure I should be hapy in such a delightful place. And happy I was, spending my days with young Em'ly, an orphan who had been taken in by Mr Peggotty.

So the fortnight slipped happily away, and at last the day came for going home. The nearer we drew the more excited I was to get there, and to run into my mother's arms. But Peggotty looked confused and out of sorts.

The door opened, and I looked for my mother. It was not she, but a strange servant.

"Why, Peggotty," I said, ruefully, "isn't she home?"

"Yes, Master Davy," said Peggotty, "and what do you think? You have got a Pa!"

I trembled, and turned white.

"A new one," said Peggotty, "come and see him." And we went to the parlour, where she left me.

On one side of the fire sat my mother; on the other, Mr Murdstone. My mother dropped her work, and arose hurriedly, but timidly.

"Now, Clara, my dear," said Mr Murdstone, "recollect! Control yourself, always control yourself! Davy boy, how do you do?"

I gave him my hand. After a moment of suspense I went and kissed my mother; she kissed me, patted me gently on the shoulder, and sat down again to her work. I could not look at her, I could not look at him, I knew quite well that he was looking at us both.

As soon as I could I crept upstairs. My old bedroom was changed, and I was to lie a long way off. This was such a miserable business that I rolled myself up in a corner of the counterpane, and cried myself to sleep.

I was awakened by my mother, followed by Mr Murdstone, who asked my mother to leave us alone. "David," he said, making his lips thin, "if I have an obstinate horse or dog to deal with, I beat him. I make him wince and smart. I say to myself: 'I'll conquer that fellow,' and I do it. And you understand me very well, I see."

9

The next evening another newcomer arrived: my new father's elder sister, a gloomy-looking lady; dark, like her brother, and with very heavy eyebrows nearly meeting over her large nose. She at once took charge of all the domestic arrangements in the house.

My lessons were held at home, always in the presence of my new father and Miss Murdstone. They were very long, very numerous, very hard lessons, and I was as much bewildered by them as my poor mother. We began badly, and went on worse.

One morning I found my mother looking anxious, Miss Murdstone looking firm, and Mr Murdstone binding something round the bottom of a cane, which he switched in the air.

My lessons having been as bad as usual, I was walked up to my room by Mr Murdstone. He had my head as in a vice, but I twined round him somehow, entreating him not to beat me. But he cut me an instant afterwards, and in the same instant I caught his hand between my teeth, and bit it through.

He beat me then as if he would have beaten me to death. Then he was gone, and the door was locked, and I was lying, fevered and hot, and torn and sore, and raging in my puny way, upon the floor.

I was imprisoned for five long days, and on the fifth night Peggotty came and told me through the keyhole that I was to be sent away to school the next morning.

In the morning Miss Murdstone told me that I was going to school and, after a short farewell from my mother and Peggotty (all that Mr Murdstone would allow), off I went.

At Yarmouth I transferred to a coach which would take me to my school, somewhere 'near London'.

Presently we arrived at Salem House, my new home. Mr Mell, one of the masters, conducted me to a door, which was opened by a stout man with a bull-neck, a wooden leg, and his hair cut close all around his head.

Salem House was a square brick building with wings, of a bare and unfinished appearance. It was so quiet that I said to Mr Mell I supposed the boys were out; but he seemed surprised at my not knowing that it was holiday-time. That all the boys were at their homes. That Mr Creakle, the proprietor, was by the seaside with Mrs and Miss Creakle. And that I was sent in holiday-time as a punishment for my misdoing.

I gazed upon the schoolroom into which he took me, seeing it as the most forlorn and desolate place I had ever seen. I see it now: long, with three rows of desks, and six of forms, and bristling round with pegs for hats and slates. Scraps of old copy-books and exercises litter the dirty floor. There is a strange unwholesome smell upon the room, like rotten books. There could not be more ink splashed about it if it had been roofless, and the skies had rained, snowed, hailed, and blown ink through the varying seasons of the year.

I came upon a placard which was lying on a desk, and bore these words: *"Take care of him. He bites"*.

"My instructions are, Copperfield," said Mr Mell, "to put this placard on your back. I am sorry, but I must do it." And with that he tied the placard on my shoulders.

My Meeting with Mr Micawber

After about a month the man with the wooden leg began to stump about with a mop and a bucket of water, from which I inferred that preparations were being made to receive Mr Creakle and the boys. I was not mistaken.

"So!" said Mr Creakle. "This is the young gentleman whose teeth are to be filed!"

Mr Creakle's face was fiery, and his eyes were small and

deep in his head; he had thick veins in his forehead, a little nose, and a large chin. "I'll tell you what I am," whispered Mr Creakle angrily. "I'm a Tartar. When I say I'll do a thing, I do it, and when I say I will have a thing done, I will have it done!" And so I became acquainted with Mr Creakle.

Soon after, I started to meet the other boys, but I was not formally received into the school until J. Steerforth arrived, for he was respected above everyone.

When he did arrive, he asked if I would like to spend some of my money on currant wine, almond cakes, biscuits and fruit. "Yes, I should like that," I said.

So, later that night, Steerforth handed round the viands. I heard all kinds of things about the school and all belonging to it; about Mr Creakle, Mr Tungay, the man with the wooden leg, Mr Mell and the other masters, and all the other boys.

The hearing of all this outlasted the banquet some time and late into the night we at last took ourselves to bed. "Goodnight, young Copperfield," said Steerforth. "I'll take care of you."

School began in earnest next day. I found that Mr Creakle was the sternest and most severe of masters, and laid about him, right and left, every day of his life.

There was just one thing for which I was grateful to Mr Creakle. One day he found my placard in his way when he came up and wanted to make a cut at me; it was taken off, and I saw it no more.

An accidental circumstance cemented the intimacy between Steerforth and me. I remarked on a certain book one day and Steerforth asked me if I had a copy. I told him no, but that it was one I had read, and he asked if I recollected them.

"Oh, yes," I replied; I had a good memory.

"Then I tell you what," said Steerforth, "you shall tell 'em to me. I can't sleep very early at night, and I wake early in the morning. We'll go over 'em one after another."

So every night and morning I would tell Steerforth the stories I had read. I was moved by no selfish motive; I admired him, and his approval was return enough.

I pass over all that happened, until my birthday came round in March, when Mrs Creakle called me to the parlour and gently told me that my beloved mother was dead.

I returned home to attend the funeral, to find comfort only in faithful old Peggotty's arms, for my new father and his sister wanted nothing to do with me.

Peggotty was given a month's notice, but as to me or my future, not a word was said. Happy they would have been, I dare say, if they could have dismissed me at a month's warning too.

I asked Peggotty what she intended to do. "I expect I shall go to Yarmouth," she replied. "But as long as you are here, I shall come over every week of my life to see you!"

And that was not all Peggotty did for me, for she asked if I might accompany her to Yarmouth for two weeks and, much to my surprise, permission was granted.

Mr Barkis, the driver, conducted us to Yarmouth, where the days passed pretty much as they had passed before.

When my visit was nearly expired, it was given out that Peggotty and Mr Barkis were going to make a day's holiday together, and that little Em'ly and I were to accompany them. The first thing we did was to stop at a church where Mr Barkis went in with Peggotty. When they returned, Mr Barkis said, "Clara Peggotty BARKIS!" and burst into a roar of laughter.

In a word , they were married. Mr and Mrs Barkis drove us back to the boat presently, bade us goodbye, and drove away to their own home.

Soon after I returned home and I fell into a solitary condition—apart from all friendly notice, apart from the society of other boys, apart from all companionship.

One day I was called before Mr Murdstone. "David," he began, "this is a world for action, not for moping and droning in, therefore I have decided that you are to take employment in the wine trade in London." And so I became, at ten years old, a little labouring hind in the service of Murdstone and Grinby.

Certain men and boys were employed to examine the wine bottles against the light, and reject those that were flawed, and to rinse and wash them. When the empty bottles ran short, there were labels to be pasted on full ones, or corks to be fitted to them, or finished bottles to be packed in casks. All this was my work.

At lunch time on my first day the manager beckoned to me to go into the counting-house, where I found a stoutish, middle-aged person, with no more hair upon his head (which was a large one and very shining) than there is upon an egg, and with a very extensive face, which he turned full upon me. He carried a jaunty sort of stick, with a large pair of rusty tassels to it; and a quizzing-glass hung outside his coat—for ornament, I afterwards found, for he very seldom looked through it, and couldn't see anything when he did.

Mr Micawber, for that was his name, said that I was to lodge with him. "My address," he said, "is Windsor Terrace, City Road. I—in short," said Mr Micawber, with a very genteel air—"I live there."

That evening he presented me to Mrs Micawber, a thin and faded lady, his twins, two other children, and the servant to the family, who informed me that she was "a Orfling" from the workhouse.

I soon found that the Micawbers were in financial difficulties, with debtors at the door at all hours of the day. Mr Micawber, was always waiting "in case anything turned up", which was his favourite expression.

At last Mr Micawber's difficulties came to a crisis, and he

was arrested and carried over to the King's Bench Prison. Soon, however, he was released, and I asked Mrs Micawber what they planned to do.

"My family are of the opinion," she answered, "that Mr Micawber should go down to Plymouth. They think that he should be on the spot."

"That he may be ready?" I suggested.

"Exactly," returned Mrs Micawber. "That he may be ready, in case of anything turning up."

The last day I spent with them was a very pleasant one, and the next morning I saw them, with a desolate heart, take their places on the coach.

I went to begin my weary day at Murdstone and Grinby's. But with no intention of passing many more weary days there. No. I resolved to run away.

My Escape to Dover

I resolved to go down into the country, to the only relation I had in the world, Miss Betsey Trotwood, my dead father's sister, who lived near Dover.

My father had been a favourite of Miss Betsey's, but my mother did not become acquainted with her until after my father's death, when she paid a surprise visit to the house.

She assured my mother that the child she expected would be a girl. "I intend to be her friend. I intend to be her godmother," she announced, and sat down to await the birth.

When told that the baby was a boy, my aunt never said a word, but took her bonnet by the strings, aimed a blow at the doctor's head with it, and walked out. She vanished and never came back any more.

I considered myself bound to finish my last week at the warehouse so, when the Saturday night came, I bade a last goodnight to my workmates, and ran away.

My box was at my old lodging and I had written on one of our address cards that we nailed on the casks: "Master David, to be left till called for, at the Coach Office, Dover". This I had in my pocket ready to put on the box, after I got it out of the house; and as I went towards my lodgings I looked for someone who would help me to carry it to the booking-office. There was a long-legged young man, with a little empty donkey-cart, and I asked him to take my box to the Dover coach office for sixpence.

"Done with you for a tanner!" he said, and rattled away at such a rate that it was as much as I could do to keep pace with the donkey.

There was a defiant manner about this young man that I did not much like; as the bargain was made, however, I took him upstairs and we brought the box down and put it on his cart. He then rattled away as if he, my box, the cart, and the donkey, were all equally mad, and I made myself quite out of breath with running and calling after him.

When I caught up with him, being much flushed and excited, I tumbled my precious half-guinea out of my pocket and put it into my mouth for safety while I tied on my address card. Suddenly I felt myself violently chucked under the chin by the young man, and saw my half-guinea fly out of my mouth into his hand. "Wot!" said the man with a frightful grin. "This is a pollis case, is it? You're a-goin to bolt, are you? Come to the pollis!" He seemed to think that I was a thief!

"You give me my money back, if you please," said I, very frightened; "and leave me alone."

"Come to the pollis!" said the young man. "You shall prove it yourn to the pollis."

The young man jumped into the cart, sat upon my box and, rattled away harder than ever.

I ran after him as fast as I could, and narrowly escaped

being run over, twenty times at least, in half a mile. Now I lost him, now I saw him, now I lost him, now I fell down in the mud, now up again, now running into somebody's arms, now running headlong at a post. At last, confused by fright and heat, I left the man to go where he would with my box and money and, panting and crying, but never stopping, faced about for Greenwich, which I had understood was on the Dover Road.

It was soon dark; I heard the clocks strike ten, as I sat resting for a while. I came upon a little shop and sold my waistcoat for ninepence, thus making my total wealth tenpence halfpenny.

I slept that night, as I was to sleep for some nights after, under the stars.

My money was short, so the next morning I sold my jacket for one shilling and fourpence.

Finally, on the sixth day of my adventure, I came upon the bare wide downs near Dover. I felt more miserable and destitute than I had done at any period of my running away. My money was all gone, I had nothing left to dispose of; I was hungry, thirsty, and worn out; and seemed as distant from the end of my struggles as ever I was.

I asked a driver if he knew my aunt, and he directed me to her house. I soon came to a very neat little cottage with cheerful bow-windows; in front of it was a small square garden full of flowers.

My shirt and trousers, stained with heat, dew, grass and soil might have frightened the birds from the garden. My hair had known no comb since I left London, and from head to foot I was powdered white with chalk and dust. I waited to introduce myself to my formidable aunt.

I was on the point of slinking off when there came out of the house a lady with her handkerchief tied over her cap, and a pair of gardening gloves on her hands, carrying a great knife. I knew her immediately to be Miss Betsey.

I went and stood beside her. "If you please, aunt," I began.

"EH?" exclaimed Miss Betsey, in a tone of amazement.

"If you please, aunt, I am your nephew, David Copperfield," I continued.

"Oh, Lord!" said my aunt. And sat flat down on the garden path.

I told her my story very briefly, and she took me into the house and sat me upon a sofa.

She called for Mr Dick, a grey-headed and florid man, whom I suspected of being a little mad, for he was always laughing without apparent reason. "This is David Copperfield," she told Mr Dick. "What shall I do with him?"

"Why, if I was you," said Mr Dick, looking vacantly at me, "I should—I should wash him!"

"Janet," said my aunt, turning to her maid, "Mr Dick sets us all right. Heat the bath!"

Janet had gone to get the bath ready, when my aunt became rigid with indignation, and cried out, "Janet! Donkeys!" Upon which, Janet came running out of the house, and warned off two donkeys that had set hoof upon a patch of green in front of the house.

I don't know whether my aunt had any lawful right-of-way over that patch of green, but whenever a donkey set foot upon it she was upon him straight away. Jugs of water were kept in secret places ready to be discharged on the offending animals and their owners; sticks were laid behind the door; sallies were made at all hours, and incessant war prevailed.

There were three such alarms before my bath was ready, and on one occasion I saw my aunt engage with a lad of fifteen, and bump his head against her own gate, before he seemed to comprehend what was the matter.

When I had bathed, I was enrobed in a shirt and trousers belonging to Mr Dick, and tied up in two or three great

shawls, and then we dined, interrupted only by my aunt's cries of: "Janet! Donkeys!"

Afterwards my aunt turned once again to Mr Dick. "What would you do with David now?" she asked.

"Oh!" said Mr Dick. "I should put him to bed."

I Go to School in Canterbury

In the morning I found my aunt musing over the breakfast table. I felt sure that I was the subject of her reflections.

"Hello!" said my aunt, after a long time. "I have written to him, your step-father."

"Oh, I can't think what I shall do," I exclaimed, "if I have to go back to Mr Murdstone!"

"I don't know anything about it," said my aunt, shaking her head. "I can't say, I am sure. We shall see."

My spirits sank under these words, and I became very downcast and heavy of heart.

At last the reply from Mr Murdstone came, and my aunt informed me, to my infinite terror, that he was coming to speak to her the next day.

The next day my aunt gave a sudden alarm of donkeys, and to my amazement I beheld Miss Murdstone ride deliberately over the sacred piece of green, and stop in front of the house.

"Go along with you!" cried my aunt. "How dare you trespass? Go along!"

My aunt paused, and I took the opportunity of telling her who the trespassers really were, but it made no difference.

"I won't be trespassed upon. I won't allow it. Go away!" she cried, and I saw a sort of hurried battle-piece, in which the donkey stood resisting everybody, while Mr Murdstone tried to lead him on, Miss Murdstone struck at Janet with a parasol, and several boys, who had come to see the engagement, shouted vigorously.

Eventually the donkey and its owner were chased off and my aunt, a little ruffled, marched past the Murdstones into the house, with great dignity, and took no notice of their presence until they were announced by Janet.

"Janet," said my aunt, "my compliments to Mr Dick, and beg him to come down." Until he came, she sat perfectly upright and stiff, then inclined her head to Mr Murdstone, who began his speech.

"Miss Trotwood," he began, "this unhappy boy has been the occasion of much domestic trouble. He has a sullen, rebellious spirit, a violent temper, and an intractable disposition. I am come here to take David back; to deal with him as I think right. Is he ready to go?"

"Are you ready to go, David?" my aunt asked me.

I answered no. I told her that they had made my mama, who always loved me dearly, unhappy about me, and I begged my aunt to befriend and protect me.

"Mr Dick," said my aunt, "what shall I do with this child?"

Mr Dick considered, hesitated, and rejoined: "Have him measured for a suit of clothes."

Miss Betsey said to Mr Murdstone: "You can go; I'll take my chance with the boy. I don't believe a word of what you have said about him." And she turned to his sister. "Let me see you ride a donkey over *my* green again, and I'll knock your bonnet off!"

Thus the Murdstones walked silently out of my life, and I began a new life with my aunt and Mr Dick. We soon became the best of friends, and they decided that I should have a new name for my new life: Trotwood Copperfield, soon shortened to Trot.

"Trot," said my aunt one evening, "we must not forget your education. Should you like to go to school at Canterbury? Tomorrow?" and I replied that I should like it.

The next morning my aunt drove her pony and trap to Canterbury, where we stopped before a very old house bulging out over the road, as if it was leaning forward.

The low arched door was opened by a youth of fifteen, whose red hair was cropped close as stubble; who had hardly any eyebrows, and no eyelashes, and eyes so unsheltered that I remember wondering how he went to sleep.

He was bony, dressed in decent black, with a white neck-cloth; and had a long, lank, skeleton hand which particularly attracted my attention.

"Is Mr Wickfield at home, Uriah Heep?" said my aunt, and we went into the house, where I was introduced to Mr Wickfield, a lawyer.

"I have brought Trot here," said my aunt, "to put him to a school where he may be well taught, and well treated. Now tell me where that school is, and all about it."

Mr Wickfield took her to the school, that she might judge it for herself, while I remained in Mr Wickfield's office.

After a pretty long absence they returned. Though the advantages of the school were undeniable, my aunt had not approved of any of the boarding-houses proposed for me.

"Well, I'll tell you what you can do, Miss Trotwood," said Mr Wickfield, "you can leave your nephew here, for the present. He won't disturb me at all. Leave him here."

And so it was agreed that I should stay in the wonderful old house. "Now, come and see my little housekeeper," said Mr Wickfield, and we went into a shady old drawing-room. He tapped at a door and a girl of about my own age came quickly out and kissed him.

This was his daughter Agnes, Mr Wickfield said. When I heard how he said it, and saw how he held her hand, I guessed what the one motive of his life was. She listened as he told her about me, and proposed that we should go upstairs and see my room. A glorious old room it was, with oak beams and diamond panes.

My aunt was as happy as I was in the arrangement. "Trot," she said, "be a credit to yourself, to me, and Mr Dick, and Heaven be with you!" And she was gone.

After dinner, we went to the drawing-room, where Mr Wickfield sat, and Agnes played on the piano, worked, and talked to him and me, until it was time for bed.

Next morning, after breakfast, I was introduced to my new master, Doctor Strong, who was in his library, his clothes not particularly well-brushed, his hair not particularly well-combed, and his shoes yawning like two caverns on the hearth-rug.

One evening, I found Uriah Heep in his office, reading a great fat book, with such attention that his lank forefinger followed every line as he read, and made clammy tracks along the page like a snail.

"I suppose you are a great lawyer?" I said.

"Me, Master Copperfield?" said Uriah. "Oh, no! I'm a very umble person. I am well aware that I am the umblest person going. My mother is likewise a very umble person. We live in an umble abode, Master Copperfield, but have much to be thankful for. If you would come and take a cup of tea at our lowly dwelling, mother would be as proud as I should be."

I said I should be glad to come, and Uriah put his book away and bade me goodnight.

In less than a fortnight at my new school I was quite at home, and happy, among my new companions. I was backward in their studies, but I went to work very hard, and gained great commendation.

Holidays by the Sea

My aunt made several excursions over to Canterbury to see me, and I saw Mr Dick every alternate Wednesday when he arrived, happy and smiling, to stay until the next morning. These Wednesdays were the happiest days of Mr Dick's life, and soon Mr Dick became a universal favourite.

One Thursday morning I met Uriah in the street, who reminded me of the promise I had made to take tea with himself and his mother.

At six o'clock, I went with Uriah to his 'umble dwelling', a house that had a bare, pinched look, where I met Mrs Heep. "This is a day to be remembered, my Uriah, I am sure," she said, "when Master Copperfield pays us a visit."

We had tea, and I found that they did just as they liked with me; and wormed things out of me about my aunt, my father, my mother, and the Wickfields. I found myself letting out things that I had no business to let out.

I had begun to be uncomfortable, when a figure looked in, and walked in, exclaiming loudly: "Copperfield!"

It was Mr Micawber! Mr Micawber, with his eyeglass, and his walking-stick, and his genteel air, all complete!

I introduced the Heeps to Mr Micawber, but I was more anxious than ever to get away. "Shall we go and see Mrs Micawber, sir?" I suggested and, to my great relief, he agreed, and took me to a little inn where they had lodgings, while they waited "for something to turn up".

That same evening it surprised me, and made me a little uneasy, to see Mr Micawber and Uriah Heep walk past, arm in arm; Uriah humbly sensible to the honour that was done him, and Mr Micawber taking a bland delight in extending his patronage to Uriah.

I did not like to say, when I dined with the Micawbers the next day, that I hoped Mr Micawber had not been too communicative with Uriah, but I was very uncomfortable about it, and often thought about it afterwards.

We had dinner at the inn, followed by hot punch. I never saw Mr Micawber such good company. As the punch disappeared, he became still more friendly, and we sang "Auld Lang Syne" together. Therefore I was not prepared for the letter which arrived the next morning from him. *"The die is cast—all is over,"* it said. *"There is no hope of the loan! The result is destruction. The bolt is impending, and the tree must fall. This is the last communication, my dear Copperfield, that you will ever receive from the beggared outcast, Wilkins Micawber"*.

I was so shocked by this heartrending letter that I ran off to offer the Micawbers a word of comfort, but halfway there I met the London coach carrying them, with Mr Micawber the very picture of tranquil enjoyment, eating walnuts, with a bottle sticking out of his breast pocket. So, with a great weight off my mind, I turned towards school.

My school days! The silent gliding on of my existence—the unseen, unfelt progress of my life—from childhood up to youth! Soon I am not the last boy in the school, and have risen over several new heads. Doctor Strong refers to me as a promising young scholar, Mr Dick is wild with joy, and my aunt remits me a guinea by the next post.

Time has stolen on unobserved—and what comes next! *I* am the head boy now! I look down on the line of boys below me, and bring to mind the boy I was myself. That little fellow seems to be no part of me; I remember him as something left behind along the road of life.

I am doubtful whether I was glad or sorry when my schooldays drew to an end and the time came for my leaving Doctor Strong's, for I had been very happy there.

For a year or more I had endeavoured to find a satisfactory answer to my Aunt Betsey's often-repeated question, "What would you like to be?" But I had no particular liking for anything.

"Trot, I tell you what, my dear," said my aunt one morning, "I think we had better take a little breathing time. Suppose you were to go down and see Peggotty again?"

"Of all things in the world, aunt, I should like it best!" I exclaimed, and plans were made.

I boarded the coach for London, and stayed at a mouldy establishment in Charing Cross.

I sat after supper and, on rising, passed a person who had come in shortly before. He did not know me, but I knew him. "Steerforth!" I cried.

"My God!" he suddenly exclaimed. "It's little Copperfield!" and we both fell at once into reminiscences of our days at Mr Creakle's.

I breakfasted with Steerforth the next morning, where I told him of my holiday. "As you are in no hurry," he said, "come home with me to Highgate, and stay a day or two." And so I did.

I spent some enjoyable days there, and at dinner one evening I said to Mrs Steerforth how glad I should be if her son would go down to Yarmouth with me.

"Should I?" said Steerforth. "Well, I think I should. It would be worth a journey." He made up his mind to go with me and the day arrived for our departure.

"Now what are you going to do?" asked Steerforth, when we were installed in the inn. "You are going to see Peggotty, I suppose? Suppose I deliver you up to be cried over for a couple of hours, and then produce myself?"

I said that it was a good idea, and went out alone to my dear old Peggotty's.

Here she was, cooking dinner! The moment I knocked at the door she opened it, and asked me what I pleased to want. I had never ceased to write to her, but it must have been seven years since we had met. "Peggotty!" I cried.

She cried, "My darling boy!" and we both burst into

tears, and were locked in one another's arms, laughing and crying at the same time. And we stayed much like this until Steerforth's arrival, when we all sat down to dinner.

He quite charmed Peggotty, until we started, at eight o'clock, for Mr Peggotty's boat. "It's Mas'r Davy!" shouted Ham, and in a moment we were all shaking hands with one another, and all talking at once.

"If this ain't," said Mr Peggotty, "the brightest night o' my life, I'm a shellfish, for just before you come in, Ham here told me that he's to marry little Em'ly!"

My Meeting with Dora Spenlow

Steerforth and I stayed for more than a fortnight. Steerforth would often go out tossing on the sea with the local fishermen, and he was sorry to have to leave "this buccaneer life". He even bought a boat which he decided to re-name *The Little Em'ly*.

While at Yarmouth, I received a letter from my aunt, asking if I should like to be a proctor. "What *is* a proctor, Steerforth?" I asked, when we were on the coach travelling back to London.

"Why, he is a sort of monkish attorney," he replied. "He is, to some faded courts held in Doctors' Commons—a lazy old nook near St Paul's churchyard—what solicitors are to the courts of law and equity." I took it to be a post connected with the legal profession.

On arriving in London I met Aunt Betsey, who had taken lodgings for a week so that we might visit the office of Messrs Spenlow and Jorkins, with whom I was to be employed, if I chose.

Mr Spenlow was a little light-haired man, with the stiffest of white cravats and shirt-collars.

It was settled that I should begin my month's probation,

and my aunt and I went off to see a furnished apartment, into which I moved the next day.

I was delighted to receive a very kind note from my dear Agnes, who was staying in London, and who asked me to go over and see her. This I did, and was sad to find her looking uneasy. She asked me if I had seen Uriah, and then astonished me by saying, "I believe he is going into partnership with Papa."

"What? Uriah? That mean, fawning fellow, worm himself into such promotion!" I cried, indignantly. "Have you made no remonstrance to your father about it, Agnes?"

"I believe it was forced upon him," said Agnes sadly.

"Forced upon him, Agnes!" I cried. "Who forced it upon him?"

"Uriah," she replied, "has made himself indispensible to Papa. He is subtle and watchful. He has mastered Papa's weaknesses and taken advantage of them until—until Papa is afraid of him."

I could do nothing to help, for Agnes begged me to be friendly to Uriah, for her father's sake, a promise that was sorely tested later when I spoke alone with Uriah and he made known to me his feelings about Agnes.

He sat, with that carved grin on his face, and told me that one day he hoped to marry Agnes!

Dear Agnes! So loving and too good for anyone that I could think of; was it possible that she was to be the wife of such a wretch as this!

Gladly, I saw no more of Uriah until the day Agnes left town. She, knowing nothing of Uriah's intentions, smiled farewell from the coach window, while he writhed on the roof, as if he already had her in his clutches.

Days and weeks slipped by, and I was asked to spend the weekend with Mr Spenlow and his family. We went into the house, and I heard a voice say, "Mr Copperfield, my daughter Dora."

Just then the dinner bell rang, and I had to go off to dress. The idea of doing anything in the way of action, in that state of love, was a little too ridiculous. I could only sit before my fire and think of the captivating, girlish, bright-eyed, lovely Dora. What a face she had, what a graceful, enchanting manner!

I was lost in a blissful delirium the whole weekend, but all too soon the time came for us to leave, and my thoughts at Doctors' Commons were of nothing but Dora.

A few days after my return, I decided to go and look after Traddles, an old friend from Salem House, for he had given me his address.

Traddles told me that he was reading for the bar, and was engaged to a curate's daughter from Devon, and boarded with the people downstairs. "Both Mr and Mrs Micawber have seen a good deal of life," he said, "and are excellent company."

I was just about to tell Traddles that I knew the Micawbers well, when in walked Mr Micawber, not a bit changed—his stick, his shirt-collar, the same as ever.

I asked Traddles and the Micawbers to dine with me, and until the day came, I lived principally on Dora and coffee. This little party was a great success. I am satisfied that Mr and Mrs Micawber could not have enjoyed the feast more, and Traddles laughed as heartily as he ate.

When they had gone, I heard other footsteps on the stairs, and recognised them as Steerforth's. "I have been seafaring in Yarmouth," he told me.

He brought a letter from Peggotty; something less legible than usual, and brief, telling me that Mr Barkis was in a hopeless state, "a little nearer" the end.

"I think I will go down and see my old nurse," I told Steerforth, but he was unwilling to let me go.

"Davy, if anything should ever separate us, you must think of me at my best, old boy," he said.

The next day I travelled to Yarmouth where I found Barkis lying unconscious. "He's a going out with the tide," said Mr Peggotty to me, and, after a long time—he did.

I passed the next week there, taking care of the will and, on the night before Peggotty and I were to leave for London, we were all to meet in the old boathouse.

Peggotty and her brother were already there when I arrived, sitting by the fireside. Soon after I sat down Mr Peggotty glanced at the clock, rose, and put a light in the window. "Theer!" he said cheerily. "Lighted up fur our little Em'ly. You see, the path ain't over light or cheerful after dark; and when I'm here at the hour as she's a comin' home, I put the light in the winder."

But it was only Ham who came and said: "Mas'r Davy, will you come out a minute?"

When we were outside I found Ham weeping. "My love, Mas'r Davy," he said, "her that I'd have died for—she's gone! Em'ly's run away!"

We broke the news to the others, and I read out the letter which Em'ly had left. "When I leave my dear home, it will be never to come back, unless he brings me back a lady," it said.

Mr Peggotty stood, long after I had ceased to read, still looking at me. Slowly he said: "Who's the man?"

"His name is Steerforth," exclaimed Ham, in a broken voice, "and he's a damned villain!"

Mr Peggotty moved no more until he seemed to wake again, all at once, and pulled down his coat from its peg in the corner.

"I'm a going to seek my niece," he said. "I'm a going to seek my Em'ly. I'm a going to find my poor niece in her shame, and bring her back. No one stop me! I'm a going to seek my niece!"

Ham spoke calmly to him, and told him that nothing could be done that night, and Mr Peggotty finally agreed to start his search the next day.

So, in the morning I was joined by Mr Peggotty and my old nurse, and we went to the coach office.

Happy Days and Sad Days

When we got to our journey's end we found lodgings for the Peggottys, and then Mr Peggotty told me that he purposed seeing Mrs Steerforth.

She was not at all sympathetic, and assured us that a marriage between her son and Emily was quite out of the question. "Such a marriage would blight my son's career, and ruin his prospects," she said.

That night after dinner, Mr Peggotty took his hat and coat, bade us goodnight, and walked out of the door. "I'm a going to seek her, fur and wide," he said, and was gone.

All this time, I had gone on loving Dora harder than ever. I was glad, therefore, when Mr Spenlow told me that this day week was Dora's birthday, and that he would be glad if I would come down and join a little picnic.

At six in the morning on the day in question I was in Covent Garden market, buying a bouquet for Dora, and at ten I was on horseback, with the bouquet in my hat, to keep it fresh, trotting down to Dora's home.

I found her sitting under a lilac tree on the lawn, in a white bonnet and a dress of celestial blue, with a great friend of hers, Julia Mills.

She was delighted with the flowers, and when she rode in front in the carriage when we set off for the picnic, often refreshed herself with their fragrance. Our eyes at those times often met; and my great astonishment is that I didn't go over the head of my gallant grey into the carriage.

The picnic was wonderful. The sun shone Dora, and the birds sang Dora. The south wind blew Dora, and the wild flowers in the hedges were all Doras. And Miss Mills understood. "Dora is coming to stay with me the day after tomorrow," she said, "if you would like to call."

When that day dawned, I was resolute to declare my passion to Dora, and know my fate. I don't know how I did it. I had Dora in my arms. Suddenly I was full of eloquence. I never stopped for a word.

I told her how I loved her. I told her I should die without her. I told her that I idolized and worshipped her. Her dog Jip barked madly all the time.

When Dora hung her head and cried my eloquence increased. If she would like me to die for her, she had but to say the word and I was ready. Life without Dora's love was not a thing to have on any terms. I couldn't bear it, and I wouldn't. I had loved her every minute, day and night, since I first saw her. The more I raved, the more Jip barked. Each of us got more mad every moment.

Well, well! Dora and I were sitting on the sofa by and by, quiet enough, and Jip was lying in her lap, winking peacefully at me. I was in a state of perfect rapture. Dora and I were engaged; secretly, of course. What a happy, foolish time it was!

One day, in my apartment, I found my aunt and Mr Dick! My aunt was sitting on a quantity of luggage, with her two birds before her, and her cat on her knee, like a female Robinson Crusoe, drinking tea! We cordially embraced.

"Trot," she said, "have you become self-reliant?"

"I think so, aunt," I answered.

"Why do you think I sit upon this property of mine tonight?"

I shook my head, unable to guess.

"Because," she said, "it's all I have. Because I'm ruined, my dear!"

How miserable I was! I thought about being poor, in Mr Spenlow's eyes, although I knew I was being selfish, thinking only of my future with Dora.

The next morning I arrived at the office early, determined to ask Mr Spenlow if he would cancel my articles and refund the premium of one thousand pounds, which my aunt had paid in kindness to me.

The proposal, however, was not acceptable to Mr Spenlow and, in a state of despondency, I went homeward. A hackney stopped before me, and occasioned me to look up. "Agnes!" I joyfully exclaimed. "Oh, dear Agnes, of all people in the world, what a pleasure to see you!"

I found that she was in London with her father and Uriah, and was on her way to my rooms to see my aunt, so we went along together.

"Your father and Heep are now partners, I suppose," I said. "Confound him! Does he still exercise the same power over Mr Wickfield?"

"There is such a change at home," said Agnes sadly, "that you would scarcely know the dear old house. The Heeps live with us now. The chief evil of their presence in the house is that I cannot watch over Papa. But if any fraud or treachery is practising against him, I only hope that simple love and truth will be stronger in the end."

Soon we reached my apartment, and we began to talk about my aunt's losses. She said that she had once had steady investments, but had thought it wiser to change them for other shares, and had lost everything.

Agnes listened with suspended breath. I thought she had some fear that her unhappy father might be in some way to blame for what had happened, but my aunt assured her that it was not his fault.

We discussed what was to be done. Agnes turned to me. "I know you would not mind," she said, "the duties of a secretary, for Doctor Strong has retired to London, and is in need of someone to help him with his work."

I was scarcely more delighted with the prospect of earning my own bread than with the hope of earning it under my old master; in short, I sat down and wrote to the Doctor, saying that I would call on him the next day.

A knock then came to the door, and I admitted Uriah Heep and Mr Wickfield, whose appearance shocked me. It was not that he looked many years older; or that there was a nervous trembling in his hand; but the fact that he should submit himself to that crawling impersonation of meanness, Uriah Heep.

"And how do you think we are looking, Mr Copperfield?" fawned Uriah. "Don't you find Mr Wickfield blooming, sir? Years don't tell in our firm, except in raising the umble, and in developing the beautiful, namely Miss Agnes."

He jerked himself about, after this compliment, in such a manner that my aunt lost all patience. "If you're an eel, sir, conduct yourself like one," she said. "If you're a man, control your limbs, sir!"

Mr Heep left soon after.

Mr Wickfield, Agnes and I had dinner together, talking about our pleasant old Canterbury days. He said it was like those good times, and he wished to Heaven they had never changed.

To see Agnes and her dear father looking so unhappy made *me* wish that things had not changed, too.

I began the next day with good resolutions. It seemed as if a complete change had come on my whole life, and with the new life, new purpose, new intention. Great was the labour; priceless the reward. Dora was the reward, and Dora must be won. And so I made my way to Doctor Strong's house.

He was happy in the prospect of our going to work together on the Dictionary (on which he had been working for as long as anyone could remember), and we settled to begin next morning at seven o'clock.

Work and Study

I was pretty busy now; up at five in the morning, and home at nine or ten at night.

One day Mr Dick and I went to visit Traddles. I had heard that many distinguished men had begun life reporting debates in Parliament, and I asked Traddles how I could qualify myself for this work. He told me that I would have to have a perfect and entire command of shorthand-writing and reading, and he looked astonished when I said: "I'll begin tomorrow."

Traddles then turned to Mr Dick. "Don't you think," he said, "you could copy writings, sir, if I got them for you?"

Mr Dick said that he could try, and by the following Saturday he had earned ten shillings and nine pence; and never shall I forget his changing this treasure into sixpences, or his bringing them to my aunt arranged in the form of a heart upon a tray, with tears of pride in his eyes.

Soon after I was invited to Mr Micawber's house, to celebrate the fact that something really had turned up at last.

I asked where he was going. "To Canterbury," he said. "I have entered into arrangements by virtue of which I stand pledged and contracted to our friend Heep, to assist and serve him in the capacity of his confidential clerk."

I stared at Mr Micawber.

"Of my friend Heep," he added, "who is a man of remarkable shrewdness, I desire to speak with all possible respect."

I sat, amazed by Mr Micawber's disclosure, and wondered just what it meant.

One Saturday evening Dora was to be at Miss Mills's, and I was to go there to tea. I had not told her of my new job.

Dora came to the drawing-room door to meet me, as

happy and loving as could be. I soon carried desolation into the bosom of our joys—not that I meant to do it—by asking Dora if she could love a beggar.

"How can you be such a silly thing," replied Dora, slapping my hand, "as to sit there, telling such stories?"

But I looked so serious that Dora left off shaking her curls, and began to cry.

"Don't talk about being poor, and working hard!" said Dora. "Oh, don't, don't! Don't be dreadful!"

At that moment, Miss Mills came into the room.

She ascertained from me in a few words what it was all about, comforted Dora, and brought us together in peace.

However, I did not allow my resolution with respect to the Parliamentary Debates, to cool. I bought an approved scheme of the art of stenography, and plunged into a sea of perplexity. The changes that were rung upon dots, that in such a position meant such a thing, and in such another position something else, entirely different; the unaccountable consequences that resulted from marks like flies' legs; all these not only troubled my waking hours, but appeared before me in my sleep.

One day, when I went to the Commons as usual, I found Mr Spenlow looking extremely grave and talking to himself. He looked at me in a distant manner, and coldly requested me to accompany him to a coffee-house. Could he have found out about my darling Dora?

In an upstairs room at the coffee-house I found Miss Murdstone, who produced from her bag my last letter to Dora, teeming with expressions of devoted affection.

"I beg to ask, Mr Copperfield, if you have anything to say about this stealthy and unbecoming action," said Mr Spenlow gravely.

"There is nothing I can say, sir," I returned, "except that all the blame is mine. Dora was induced and persuaded by me to consent to this concealment, and I bitterly regret it."

"It is nonsense," Mr Spenlow went on. "Our future intercourse must be restricted to the Commons here, and we will agree to make no further mention of the past. All I desire, Mr Copperfield, is that it should be forgotten."

I confided all to my aunt when I got home; and went to bed despairing. I got up despairing, and went out despairing, straight to the Commons.

The clerks were there, but nobody was doing anything.

"This is a dreadful calamity," said one of them.

"What is?" I exclaimed. "What's the matter?"

"Mr Spenlow," said another. "Dead!"

After about six weeks, I had still heard nothing from Dora, but Julia Mills informed me that she had gone to live at Putney with her two aunts, maiden sisters of Mr Spenlow. I did not know if I would ever see her dear face again.

My aunt—beginning, I imagine, to be made seriously uncomfortable by my prolonged dejection—made a pretence of being anxious that I should go to Dover to see that all was well at the cottage, which was let.

I found everything satisfactory and was enabled to gratify my aunt by reporting that the tenant inherited her feud, and waged incessant war against the donkeys.

Having settled the business I had there, I walked on to Canterbury, to Mr Wickfield's house.

There I found Mr Micawber, plying his pen with great assiduity. He was dressed in a legal-looking suit of black, and loomed, burly and large, in the small office. He seemed well pleased with his new occupation, though I saw an uneasy change in him.

Then I looked into Agnes's room. What a pleasure to be the cause of that bright change in her attentive face, and the object of that welcome!

I poured out all my troubles and problems to her, and asked her what I should do.

"I think," said Agnes, "that the honourable course to take would be to write to those two ladies." I wrote that very afternoon.

The evening was spent under the ever-watchful eye of Mrs Heep, and the whole of the next day. I had not an opportunity of speaking to Agnes, and finally went out by myself.

I had not walked far when I was hailed by someone behind me. The shambling figure, and the scanty great-coat, were not to be mistaken. Uriah Heep came up.

He seemed intent on reminding me of his regard for Agnes, and seemed worried that I might be a rival for her hand. I assured him that I was engaged to another young lady.

After dinner he insisted that I should go into the study with Mr Wickfield and himself.

Uriah proposed a toast to Agnes. "Agnes Wickfield is," he said, "the divinest of her sex. To be her father is a proud distinction, but to be her husband—"

Spare me from ever again hearing such a cry as that with which her father rose up from the table!

"What's the matter?" said Uriah, turning a deadly colour. "You are not gone mad, I hope? If I say I've an ambition to make *your* Agnes *my* Agnes, I have as good a right to it as another man!"

Mr Wickfield was mad for a moment, tearing out his hair, beating his head; then he pointed to Uriah. "Look at my torturer," said Mr Wickfield. "Before him I have aban-doned name and reputation, peace and quiet, house and home. I have brought misery on the one I dearly love!"

My Marriage

In the morning I took the coach back to London, and spent an anxious time awaiting a reply from Dora's aunts.

At last an answer came. They said that if Mr Copperfield would call, they would be happy to hold some conversation upon the subject of their niece.

Traddles was to accompany me, and on the appointed day I found myself backing into the fireplace, and bowing in great confusion to two dry little elderly ladies, dressed in black.

When I had sat upon something which was not a cat—my first seat was—I so far recovered my sight as to perceive that Mr Spenlow had evidently been the youngest of the family.

The two sisters, Miss Lavinia and Miss Clarissa, were not unlike birds; having a sharp, brisk, sudden manner, and a little short, spruce way of adjusting themselves, like canaries.

"You ask permission of my sister Clarissa and myself," said Miss Lavinia, "to visit here, as the accepted suitor of our niece?"

I confirmed this and was delighted when they said that I was to be allowed to visit Dora!

I was reunited with my darling Dora, and we spent many happy hours together with the aunts, planning our wedding.

Soon after, Agnes and her father came on a visit, and I took her to see Dora. I never was so pleased as when I saw those two sit down together, side by side.

When it was time for Agnes to leave there was a hurried but affectionate parting between them; and Dora was to write to Agnes, and Agnes was to write to Dora.

Weeks, months, seasons, pass along. I have attained the dignity of twenty-one. Let me think what I have achieved.

I have tamed the savage stenographic mystery; I make a respectable income by it. I am in high repute for my accomplishment in reporting the debates in Parliament for a morning newspaper.

I have come out in another way. I have taken to authorship. I wrote a little something, in secret, and sent it to a magazine, and it was published. Since then, I have written a good many pieces. I am regularly paid for them. Altogether, I am well off.

We have removed to a very pleasant little cottage. My aunt, however, is not going to remain here, but intends removing herself to a still more tiny cottage close at hand. What does this portend? My marriage? Yes!

Yes! I am going to be married to Dora! Miss Lavinia and Miss Clarissa have given their consent; and if ever canary birds were in a flutter, they are.

At last the great day dawns, and I get up very early to fetch my aunt.

I have never seen my aunt in such state. She is dressed in lavender-coloured silk, and has a white bonnet on, and is amazing. Peggotty is ready to go to church, intending to behold the ceremony from the gallery. Mr Dick, who is to give my darling to me at the altar, has had his hair curled. Traddles presents a dazzling combination of cream colour and light blue.

The rest is all a more a less incoherent dream. A dream of Agnes taking care of Dora; of my aunt with tears rolling down her face; of little Dora trembling very much, and making her responses in faint whispers.

Of our kneeling down together, side by side; of the service being got through, quietly and gravely; of its being over, and our going away. Of our all being so merry and talkative in the carriage going back.

Dora and I drive away together, and I awake from the dream. I believe it at last. It is my dear, dear, little wife beside me, whom I love so well!

It was a strange condition of things, the honeymoon being over, when I found myself sitting down in my own house with Dora.

I doubt whether two young birds could have known less about keeping house, than I and my pretty Dora did. We had a servant, of course. She kept house for us, but we had an awful time of it with Mary Anne.

"Don't you think, my dear," I said to Dora one evening when dinner was late again, "it would be better for you to remonstrate with Mary Anne?"

"Oh no, please! I couldn't, Doady!" said Dora. "Don't be a naughty Blue Beard! Don't be serious!"

Mary Anne left, after having borrowed little sums from the local tradespeople in my name, to be followed by a long line of Incapables.

Everybody we had anything to do with seemed to cheat us. Our appearance in a shop was a signal for the damaged goods to be brought out immediately. All our meat turned out to be tough, and there was hardly any crust on our loaves.

It appeared to me, on looking over the tradesmen's books, as if we kept the basement paved with butter, such was the extensive scale of our consumption of that article. As to the washer-woman pawning the clothes, and coming in a state of penitent intoxication to apologise, I suppose that might have happened to anybody.

One of our first feats of housekeeping was dinner for Traddles. I could not have wished for a prettier little wife at the opposite end of the table, but I certainly could have wished that Jip had never been encouraged to walk about the table-cloth during dinner, especially as he had a habit of putting his foot in the melted butter. On this occasion he seemed to think that he was to keep Traddles at bay; and he barked at him and made short runs at his plate.

Dora had bought oysters but had forgotten to have them opened; so we looked at the oysters and ate the mutton. At least we ate as much of it as was done.

When Traddles went away, my wife sat down by my side. "I am very sorry," she said. "Will you try to teach me, Doady?"

I did try, and Dora told me that she was going to be a wonderful housekeeper. She bought an account-book, and made quite a desperate attempt to "be good" as she called it. But when she had entered two or three laborious items, Jip would walk over the page, wagging his tail, and smear them all out. Her own little finger got steeped to the bone in ink; and I think that was the only result obtained.

Thus it was that I took upon myself the toils and cares of our life, and Dora was bright and cheerful in the old childish way.

Mr Micawber's Secret

I must have been married about a year when one evening I came past Mrs Steerforth's house, and was surprised when I was beckoned inside by the maid.

I was told that Emily had run away from James Steerforth in Naples, where they had been living, and that nothing had been seen or heard of her since.

I felt it should be communicated to Mr Peggotty. On the following evening I went in quest of him. He was always wandering about from place to place, with his one object of finding his niece before him. Often I had seen him passing along the streets, searching among the few who loitered out of doors at those untimely hours, for what he dreaded to find.

He was much changed; his hair was long and ragged, his face burnt dark by the sun, for he had travelled far away in his search. He was greyer, the lines in his face and fore-head were deeper, but he looked very strong, like a man whom nothing could tire out.

He looked intently at me, and listened in profound silence to all I had to tell. "My niece, Em'ly, is alive, sir!" he said at length. He looked like a man inspired, and deter-mined to search the whole of London, for we thought it the place to which she would eventually return.

I laboured hard at the book I was writing, without allow-ing it to interfere with my newspaper duties; and it came out and was very successful.

We had by this time given up the housekeeping as a bad job. The house kept itself, and we kept a page. His princi-pal function was to quarrel with the cook.

He appears to have lived in a hail of saucepan-lids. He would shriek for help and come tumbling out of the kitchen, with iron missiles flying after him. I wanted to get rid of him, but could not do so until one day he stole Dora's watch.

As our second year together wore on, Dora was not strong, and was confined to bed for short periods. I began to carry her downstairs every morning, and upstairs every night. We thought she would be "running about as she used to do" in a few days. But they said, wait a few days more, and then, wait a few days more; and still she neither ran nor walked.

I received one morning a letter from Mr Micawber, asking Traddles and I to meet him.

I heard from Traddles that he had had a letter from Mrs Micawber, saying that she was worried about her husband, asking him "to step in between Mr Micawber and his agonized family".

Mr Micawber was more confused and less genteel than of yore. He seemed in very low spirits, and was not his usual self at all.

He rode to my aunt's house with us, although for the better part of the journey he was plunged into deep gloom.

Mr Dick was at home. He was by nature so exceedingly compassionate of anyone who seemed to be ill at ease, that he shook hands with Mr Micawber at least half a dozen times in five minutes.

"The friendliness of this gentleman," said Mr Micawber, "if you will allow me to cull a figure of speech from the vocabulary of our coarser national sports—floors me."

"My friend Mr Dick," replied my aunt, proudly, "is not a common man."

"That I am convinced of," said Mr Micawber, for Mr Dick was shaking hands with him again.

I asked Mr Micawber if he would make some punch (his great speciality) for us, but his thoughts seemed to be elsewhere. I saw him putting the lemon-peel into the kettle, the sugar into the snuffer-tray, the spirit into the empty jug, and he confidently attempted to pour boiling water out of a candlestick. I saw that a crisis was at hand, and it came. He clattered all his implements together, rose from his chair, and burst into tears.

"Mr Micawber," said I, "what is the matter?"

"What is the matter, gentlemen?" asked Mr Micawber. "Villainy is the matter; deception, fraud, conspiracy, are the matter; and the name of the whole atrocious mass is—HEEP! I will lead this life no longer. I'll put my hand in no man's hand until I have—blown to fragments—the—a—detestable—serpent—HEEP! Refreshment—a—underneath this roof—particularly punch—would—a—choke me—unless—I had—previously—choked the eyes—out of the head —a—of—interminable cheat, and liar—HEEP!"

I had some fear of Mr Micawber's dying on the spot. I would have gone to his assistance, but he waved me off.

"No, Copperfield! he gasped. "No communication—a—until—this day week—a—at breakfast time—a—everybody present—at the hotel in Canterbury—a—where—Mrs Micawber and I—will expose intolerable ruffian—HEEP! No more to say—go immediately—upon the track of devoted and doomed traitor—HEEP!"

With this Mr Micawber rushed out of the house.

By this time, some months had passed since I had seen Mr Peggotty, and I did not know that any clue had been obtained as to Emily's fate. I confess that I began to sink deeper and deeper into the belief that she was dead.

Out in the garden one evening I was surprised to see Martha, who had known Emily in Yarmouth, and was helping Mr Peggotty in his search, beckoning to me.

I followed her to a poor lodging house, and we proceeded to the top of the house, where I heard a soft voice. It was Emily's! Then Mr Peggotty rushed into the room.

"Uncle!"

A fearful cry followed the word. I paused a moment and, looking in, saw him supporting her insensible figure in his arms.

"Mas'r Davy," he said, "I thank my Heav'nly Father as my dream's come true!"

With those words he took her up in his arms and carried her, motionless and unconscious, down the stairs.

The next day Mr Peggotty told me Emily's story; how, when she escaped from the villa, she lived with a fisherman's family; how she then travelled to France and earned enough for her passage to Dover by serving in an inn; and how she was finally set ashore at Dover.

"You have made up your mind," said I to Mr Peggotty, "as to the future, good friend?"

"Quite, Mas'r Davy," he returned, "and told Em'ly. Theer's mighty countries, fur from heer. Our future life lays over the sea."

"They will emigrate together, Aunt Betsey," said I.

"Yes!" said Mr Peggotty, with a hopeful smile. "No one can't reproach my darling in Australia. We will begin a new life over theer."

And so Mr Peggotty made happy preparations for their departure.

When the time Mr Micawber had appointed for our meeting came, my aunt, Mr Dick, Traddles and I went down to the hotel in Canterbury.

"Now, sir," said my aunt to Mr Micawber, "we are ready as soon as you please."

"Well," said Mr Micawber, "I would beg to be allowed a start of five minutes by the clock; and then to receive the present company, inquiring for Miss Wickfield, at the office of Wickfield and Heep, whose Stipendiary I am."

My aunt and I looked at Traddles, who nodded his approval.

When the time was expired, we all went out together to the old house without saying one word on the way.

Uriah is Undone

We found Mr Micawber at his desk, either writing, or pretending to write, hard. I asked if Miss Wickfield was at home.

Mr Micawber preceded us and, flinging open the door of Mr Wickfield's former office, said, in a sonorous voice: "Miss Trotwood, Mr David Copperfield, Mr Thomas Traddles, and Mr Dixon!"

Our visit astonished Uriah Heep, but his astonishment lasted only a moment, and afterwards he was as fawning and as humble as ever.

Agnes was ushered in by Mr Micawber, and Traddles, unobserved, went out.

Mr Micawber, with a large office ruler at his breast, stood erect before the door.

"What are you waiting for?" said Uriah. "Micawber! Did you hear me tell you not to wait?"

"Yes!" replied the immovable Mr Micawber.

"Then why *do* you wait?" said Uriah.

"Because I—in short, choose," replied Mr Micawber, with a burst.

Uriah's cheeks lost colour, and an unwholesome paleness, still faintly tinged by his pervading red, overspread them.

"If there is a scoundrel on this earth," continued Mr Micawber with the utmost vehemence, "that scoundrel's name is—HEEP!"

Uriah fell back, as if he had been struck or stung. Looking slowly round upon us with the darkest and wickedest expression that his face could wear, he said, in a lower voice: "Oho! This is a conspiracy! You have met here by appointment! You envy me my rise, do you?"

Just then, Traddles returned with Mrs Heep. "And what do you want here?" asked Uriah.

"I have a power of attorney from Mr Wickfield in my pocket," said Traddles in a composed, businesslike way, "to act for him in all matters."

Mr Micawber now burst forward, drew the ruler from his breast, and produced from his pocket a foolscap document, and began to read the letter with great relish. "In an accumulation of Ignominy, Want, Despair, and Madness," he read, "I entered the firm nominally conducted under the appellation of Wickfield and—HEEP, but in reality, wielded by—HEEP alone. HEEP, and only HEEP, is the mainspring of that machine. HEEP, and only HEEP, is the Forger and the Cheat."

Uriah, more blue than white, made a dart at the letter, as if to tear it to pieces. Mr Micawber caught his advancing knuckles with the ruler, and disabled his right hand.

"Approach me again, you—you—you HEEP of infamy," gasped Mr Micawber, "and if your head is human, I'll break it!"

Mr Micawber, when he was sufficiently cool, then proceeded. He told us that, "Mr W. was imposed upon, kept in ignorance, and deluded, in every possible way." That Heep had obtained large sums of money from Mr Wickfield by false pretences. That Heep had many times forged the signature of Mr Wickfield, in Mr Micawber's presence, and that Heep had even forced Mr Wickfield to relinquish his share of the partnership. Of all these charges Mr Micawber had proof, he said.

There was an iron safe in the room. The key was in it. Uriah went to it and threw the doors open. It was empty.

"Where are the books?" he cried, with a frightful face. "Some thief has stolen the books!"

Mr Micawber tapped himself with the ruler. "*I* did, when I got the key from you as usual this morning."

"Well, what do you want done?" asked Uriah with a ferocious look.

"First, the deed of relinquishment must be given over to me," said Traddles calmly, "then you must prepare to make restoration to the last farthing. All the books and papers must remain in our possession; all money accounts and securities. In short, everything here. In the meanwhile, and until everything is done to our satisfaction, we compel you to keep to your own room, and hold no communication with anyone."

Uriah, without lifting his eyes from the ground, shuffled across the room with his hand to his chin, and was gone.

Happiness restored, my aunt turned to Mr Micawber. "I wonder you have never turned your thoughts to emigration," she said.

"Madam," returned Mr Micawber, "it was the dream of

my youth, and the aspiration of my riper years."

"But are the circumstances of Australia such that a man of Mr Micawber's abilities would have a chance of rising in the social scale?" asked Mrs Micawber, who had just arrived.

"There are no better openings anywhere," said my aunt, "for a man who conducts himself well, and is industrious."

"For a man who conducts himself well," repeated Mrs Micawber, "and is industrious. Precisely. It is evident to me that Australia is the legitimate sphere of action for Mr Micawber."

And so it was settled; the Micawbers were to emigrate to Australia, with a loan from my aunt.

I must pause yet again. I am again with Dora, in our cottage. I do not know how long she has been ill. It is not really long, in weeks or months; but it is a weary, weary while.

They have left off telling me to "wait a few days more". I have begun to fear, remotely, that the day may never shine when I shall see my child-wife running in the sunlight with her old friend Jip, who is suddenly grown very old now.

Dora lies smiling on us, and is beautiful, and utters no hasty or complaining word. Agnes is with us, and one evening Dora asks if I will send her up.

I give her the message and she disappears, leaving me alone with Jip.

How the time wears I know not, until I am recalled by my child-wife's old companion. More restless than he was, he looks at me, and wanders to the door, and whines to go upstairs.

"Not tonight, Jip! Not tonight!"

He comes very slowly to me, licks my hand, and lifts his dim eyes to my face. He lies down at my feet, stretches himself out as if to sleep, and with a plaintive cry, is dead.

"Oh, Agnes! Look, look, here!" I say as she enters the room.

That face, so full of pity, and of grief, that rain of tears, that awful mute appeal to me, that solemn hand upraised towards Heaven!

"Agnes?"

It is over. Darkness comes before my eyes; and, for a time, all things are blotted out of my remembrance.

This is not the time at which I am to enter on the state of my mind beneath its load of sorrow. An interval occurred before I fully knew my own distress, an interval during which I had to see the emigrants safely on their voyage, and the "final pulverization of Heep", as Mr Micawber called it.

At the request of Traddles, we all soon returned to Canterbury, to be told that all the money had been recovered, and that Uriah and his mother had left for London. Agnes was to start a school in the old house, and my aunt now had enough money to return to her house in Dover.

I received a letter for Ham from Emily, and decided to take it down to Yarmouth myself.

I went down on the coach. There had been a wind all day and it was rising with an extraordinary great sound. As the night advanced, it came on to blow harder and harder. It still increased, until our horses could scarcely face the wind. As we struggled on into Yarmouth, nearer and nearer to the sea, from which this mighty wind was blowing dead on shore, its force became more and more terrific. Long before we saw the sea its spray was on our lips and showered salt rain upon us.

The tremendous sea itself—when I could find sufficient pause to look at it, in the agitation of the blinding wind, the flying stones and sand, and the awful noise—confounded me.

I learned that Ham had gone to Lowestoft on business,

and so I went back to the inn, where I spent a restless night, only to be awakened by someone knocking and calling at my door.

"What is the matter?" I cried.

"A wreck! Close by! A schooner from Spain or Portugal, laden with fruit and wine."

I ran down to the beach where I saw it, close in upon us! One mast was broken short off, and lay over the side, as the ship rolled and beat. Then suddenly the sea, sweeping over the rolling wreck, made a clean breach, and carried men, casks, planks into the boiling surge.

Four men only arose from the wreck out of the deep, clinging to the rigging of the remaining mast; uppermost, an active figure with long curling hair, conspicuous among the rest. Again we lost her, and again she rose. Two men were gone. The agony on shore increased. Men groaned, and clasped their hands; women shrieked, and turned away their faces. Some ran wildly up and down along the beach, crying for help where no help could be.

I saw the people part, and Ham came breaking through to the front. I held him back with both arms, and implored the sailors not to let him stir off that sand! But he was determined, and soon I saw him standing alone, a rope in his hand; another round his body; and several of the best men holding firmly to the latter.

Ham watched until there was a great retiring wave, when he dashed in after it, and in a moment was buffeting with the water; rising with the hills, falling with the valleys, lost beneath the foam; then drawn again to land. They hauled in hastily.

He was hurt, but he took no thought of that, and was gone as before. And now he made for the wreck. At length he neared the wreck. He was so near that, with one more of his vigorous strokes he would be clinging to it—when a high, green, vast hillside of water came moving on shoreward from beyond the ship; he seemed to leap up into it with a mighty bound, and the ship was gone!

They drew him to my very feet—insensible—dead. He had been beaten to death by the great wave.

As I sat later a fisherman asked me to go with him. He led me to the shore where—among the ruins of the home he had wronged—I saw Steerforth lying with his head upon his arm, as I had often seen him lie at school.

We took our burden to the inn, and I left for London that same night, where I broke the news of her son's death to Mrs Steerforth.

One thing more I had to do, before yielding myself to the shock of these events. It was to conceal what had occurred from those who were going away, and to dismiss them on their voyage in happy ignorance.

We had a small farewell party for the voyagers, and the next day my old nurse and I went down to Gravesend where we bade a fond farewell to Mr Peggotty, Emily and all the Micawbers.

On deck, I told Mr Peggotty of the noble spirit that had gone, and wrung his hand; and if ever I have loved and honoured any man, I loved and honoured that man in my soul.

We went over the side into our boat, and lay at a little distance to see the ship wafted on her course.

I went away from England; leaving all who were dear to me. I roamed from place to place, carrying my burden of sorrow with me everywhere. I went from city to city, seeking I know not what, and trying to leave I know not what behind.

A letter was waiting for me in Switzerland. I opened it, and read the writing of Agnes. She was happy and useful, and was prospering as she had hoped. That was all she told me of herself. The rest referred to me. She gave me no advice; she urged no duty on me; she only told me, in her own fervent manner, what her trust in me was. I put the letter to my breast, and thought what I had been an hour ago!

I did glance to a period when I might possibly be so blessed as to marry her. But, as time wore on, this shadowy prospect faded. If she had ever loved me, could I believe that she would love me now?

Three years had elapsed since the sailing of the emigrant ship, when, at the same hour of sunset, and in the same place, I stood on the vessel that brought me home.

I Find Happiness Again

I landed in London on a wintry autumn evening. My first

call was on Traddles. "Good God!" he cried. "It's Copper-field!" and rushed into my arms. "To think you should have been so nearly coming home and not at the cere-mony!"

"What ceremony?" I asked.

"Why, my dear Copperfield," said Traddles, "I am married!"

And to my amazement, the "dearest girl in the world" came out at that same instant, laughing and blushing, and I spent a very happy evening with them both.

I passed the next day on the Dover coach; burst safe and sound into my aunt's parlour while she was at tea (she wore spectacles now); and was received by her, and Mr Dick, and dear old Peggotty, who acted as housekeeper.

My aunt and I, when we were left alone, talked far into the night. How the emigrants wrote cheerfully and hope-fully; how Mr Dick occupied himself by copying everything he could lay his hands on; and that Janet was happily married.

"And when, Trot," said my aunt, "are you going over to Canterbury? You will find Mr Wickfield a white-haired old man, and you will find Agnes as good, as beautiful, as earnest, as she has always been."

I answered that I would go over in the morning.

I was shown up the grave old staircase into the unchanged drawing-room. All the changes that had crept in when the Heeps were there, were changed again. Everything was as it used to be, in the happy time.

The opening of the little door in the panelled wall made me start and turn. Her beautiful serene eyes met mine as she came towards me. I caught her in my arms.

I folded her to my heart, and for a little while, we were both silent. She was so true, she was so beautiful, she was so good—I owed her so much gratitude, she was so dear to me, that I could find no utterance for what I felt.

I spent the rest of the day walking through the streets of my childhood, and returned to the house for dinner with Agnes and her father.

For a time—until my new book should be completed, which would be the work of several months—I took up my abode in my aunt's house at Dover.

Occasionally I went to London; to lose myself in the swarm of life there, or to consult with Traddles on some business point. He had managed well for me and my worldly affairs were prospering. As my notoriety as an author began to bring upon me an enormous quantity of letters, I arranged to have them delivered to Traddles' address, where I laboured through them periodically.

One of these letters was from Mr Creakle, our old schoolmaster from so long ago, who told me that he was now a Middlesex Magistrate in charge of a prison. He asked if Traddles and I would visit him there, and the next day we went down together.

Mr Creakle was not much changed in appearance, but his welcome was. He received me like a man who had formed my mind in bygone years, and had always loved me dearly. He took us on a tour of the prison. His model prisoner was known as Number Twenty Seven. At last we came to the door of his cell, and Mr Creakle directed that the door should be opened, and Twenty Seven be invited out into the passage. Whom should Traddles and I behold but Uriah Heep!

He said with the old writhe: "How do you do, Mr Copperfield? How do you do, Mr Traddles?"

When he had assured the visitors of how penitent he was, and how happy he was in their prison, he sneaked back into his cell, and both Traddles and I experienced a great relief when he was locked in.

The year came round to Christmas-time, and I had been at home about two months. I had seen Agnes frequently.

At least once a week, sometimes oftener, I rode over there, and passed the evening. She did not show me any change in herself. What she always had been to me, she still was; wholly unaltered.

As I sat with Agnes I decided that I had to know how she felt about me. I could no longer pretend that I still looked on her as a sister.

"Dearest Agnes!" I burst out. "Whom I so respect and honour—whom I so devotedly love! When I came here today, I thought that nothing could have wrested this confession from me. But, Agnes, if I have any hope that I may ever call you something more than Sister, widely different from Sister!—"

Agnes was weeping, but not sadly—joyfully! And clasped in my arms as she had never been, as I had thought she never was to be!

"I went away," I said, "dear Agnes, loving you. I stayed away, loving you. I returned home, loving you!"

"I am so blest, Trotwood," said Agnes, her sweet eyes shining through her tears, "my heart is so over-charged—but there is one thing I must say."

"Dearest, what?" I asked.

"I have loved you all my life!"

Oh, we were happy, we were happy! And so was my aunt when we broke the news to her! And Mr Dick and Peggotty!

We were married within a fortnight. We left our guests full of joy and drove away together. "Dearest husband!" said Agnes. "I have one more thing to tell you. It grows out of the night when Dora died. She told me that she made a last request to me, and left me a last charge, that only I would occupy this vacant place."

What I have purposed to record is nearly finished; but there is yet one incident, without which one thread in the web I have spun would have a ravelled end.

I have advanced in fame and fortune, my domestic joy was perfect, I had been married ten happy years. Agnes and I were sitting in our house in London, one night in spring, and three of our children were playing in the room, when I was told that a stranger wished to see me.

It was Mr Peggotty! An old man now, but in a ruddy, hearty, strong old age. When our first emotion was over, and he sat before the fire with the children on his knees, and the blaze shining on his face, he looked, to me, as vigorous and robust an old man as ever I had seen.

"It's a mort of water," said Mr Peggotty, "fur to come across, and on'y stay a matter of fower weeks. But water ('specially when 'tis salt) comes nat'ral to me; and friends is dear, and I am heer—which is verse, though I hadn't such intentions. Our fortuns is soon told. We haven't fared no hows, but fared to thrive. We've allus thrived. What with sheep-farming, and what with stock-farming, and what with one thing and what with t'other, we are as well to do, as well could be."

"And Emily?" said Agnes and I, both together.

"Em'ly," replied Mr Peggotty, "is cheerful along with me; retired when others is by; fond of going any distance fur to teach a child, or fur to tend a sick person; fondly loving of her uncle; patient; liked by young and old; sowt out by all that has any trouble. That's Em'ly!"

When I asked of Mr Micawber, Mr Peggotty produced a little odd-looking newspaper, where we read of *our distinguished fellow-colonist and townsman, WILKINS MICAWBER, ESQUIRE, Port Middlebay District Magistrate.*

We talked much of Mr Micawber and his rise to fame. Mr Peggotty lived with us during his stay, and his sister and my aunt came to London to see him. Agnes and I parted from him aboardship, when he sailed; and we shall never part from him more on earth.

And now my written story ends. I look back, once more—for the last time—before I close these leaves.

I see myself, with Agnes at my side, journeying along the road of life. I see our children and our friends around us.

What faces are the most distinct to me in the crowd? Here is my aunt, in stronger spectacles, an old woman of fourscore years and more, but upright yet, and a steady walker of six miles at a stretch in winter weather. Always with her, here comes Peggotty, my good old nurse, likewise in spectacles, accustomed now to doing her needlework at night very close to the lamp.

Among my boys I see an old man making giant kites with a delight for which there are no words. He greets me rapturously, and whispers, with many nods and winks: "Trotwood, you will be glad to hear that your aunt's the most extraordinary woman in the world, sir!"

And lo, the Doctor, always our good friend, labouring at his Dictionary (somewhere about the letter D), and happy in his home and wife.

Working at his chambers in a lawyer's wig, I come upon my dear old Traddles, exactly the same simple, unaffected fellow as he ever was.

And now, as I close my task, subduing my desire to linger yet, these faces fade away. But one face, shining on me like a Heavenly light by which I see all other objects, is above them and beyond them all. And that remains.

I turn my head, and see it, in its beautiful serenity, beside me. My lamp burns low, and I have written far into the night; but the dear presence, without which I were nothing, bears me company.

Oh Agnes, oh my soul, so may thy face be by me when I close my life indeed; so may I, when realities are melting from me like the shadows which I now dismiss, still find thee near me, pointing upward!